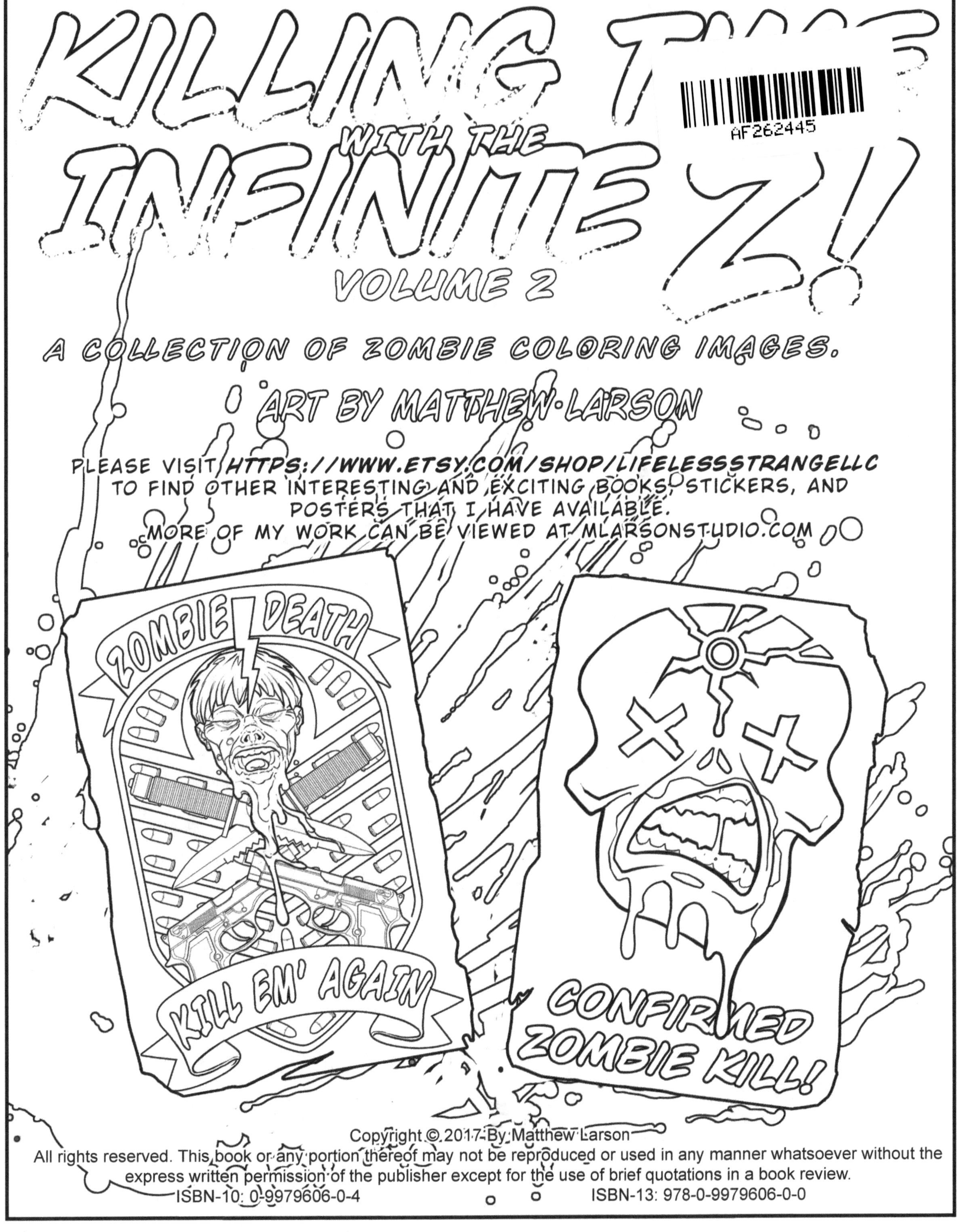

KILLING TIME
WITH THE
INFINITE Z!
VOLUME 2
A COLLECTION OF ZOMBIE COLORING IMAGES.
ART BY MATTHEW LARSON
PLEASE VISIT HTTPS://WWW.ETSY.COM/SHOP/LIFELESSSTRANGELLC
TO FIND OTHER INTERESTING AND EXCITING BOOKS, STICKERS, AND
POSTERS THAT I HAVE AVAILABLE.
MORE OF MY WORK CAN BE VIEWED AT MLARSONSTUDIO.COM
AF262445
ZOMBIE DEATH
KILL EM' AGAIN
CONFIRMED
ZOMBIE KILL!

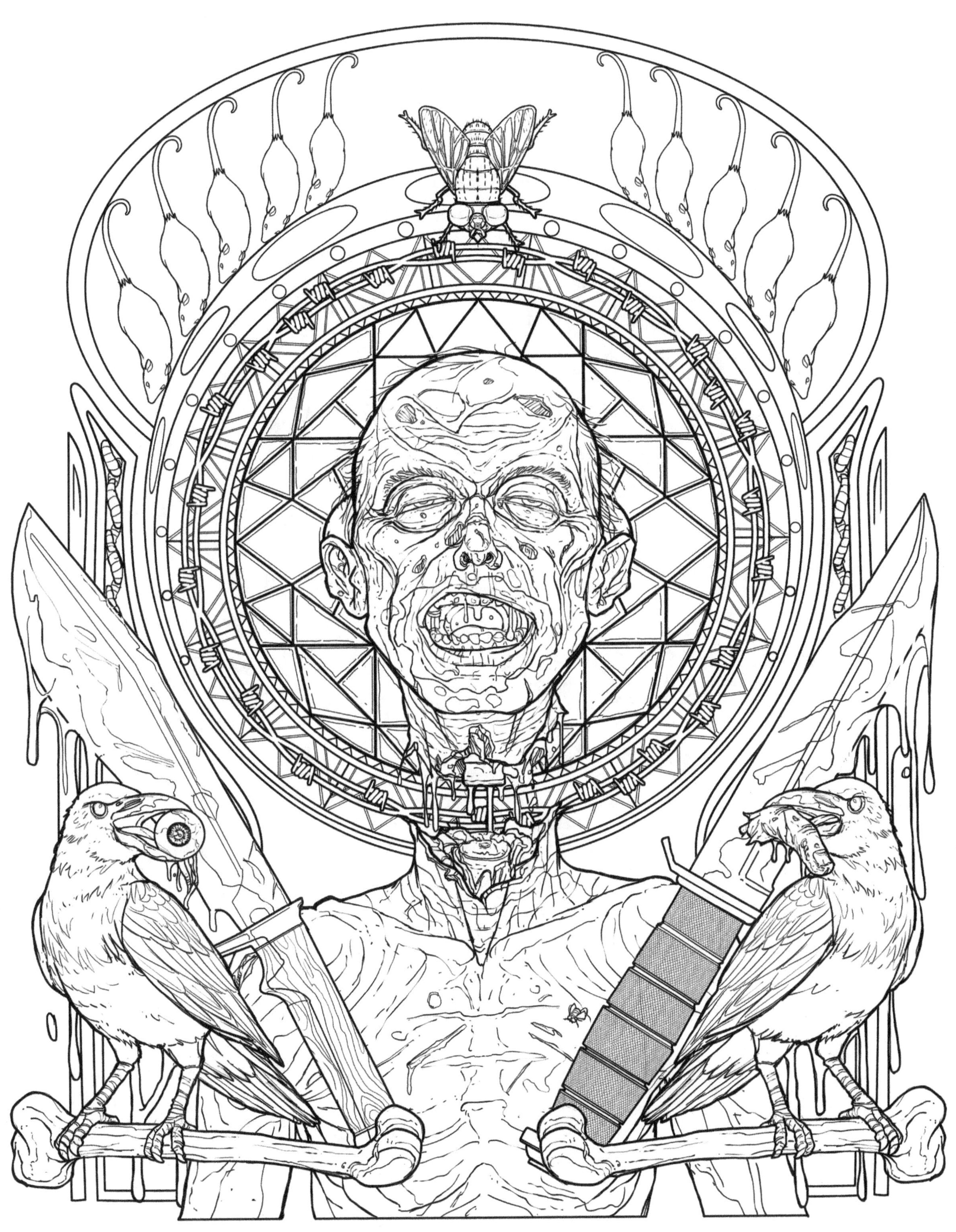

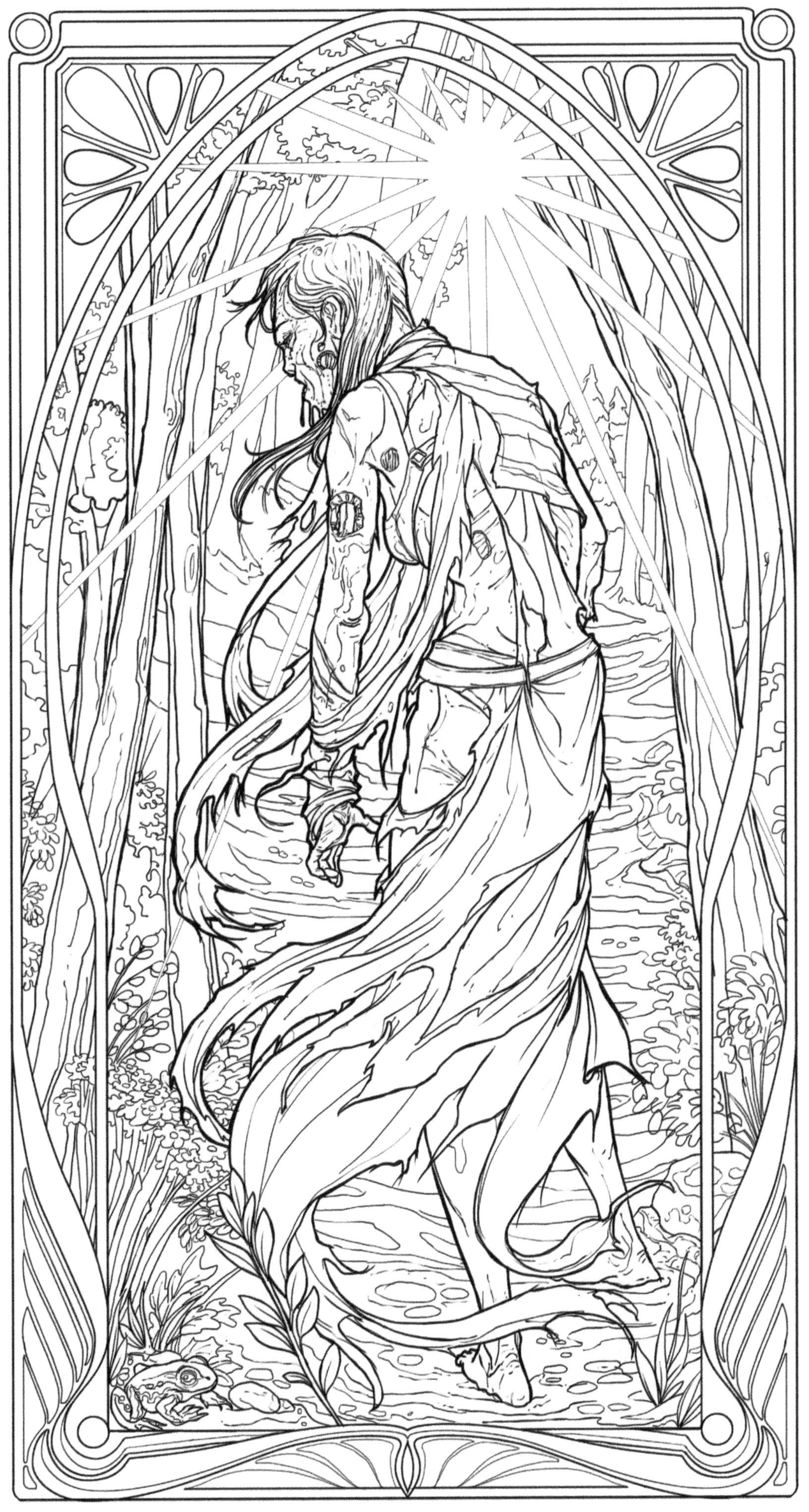

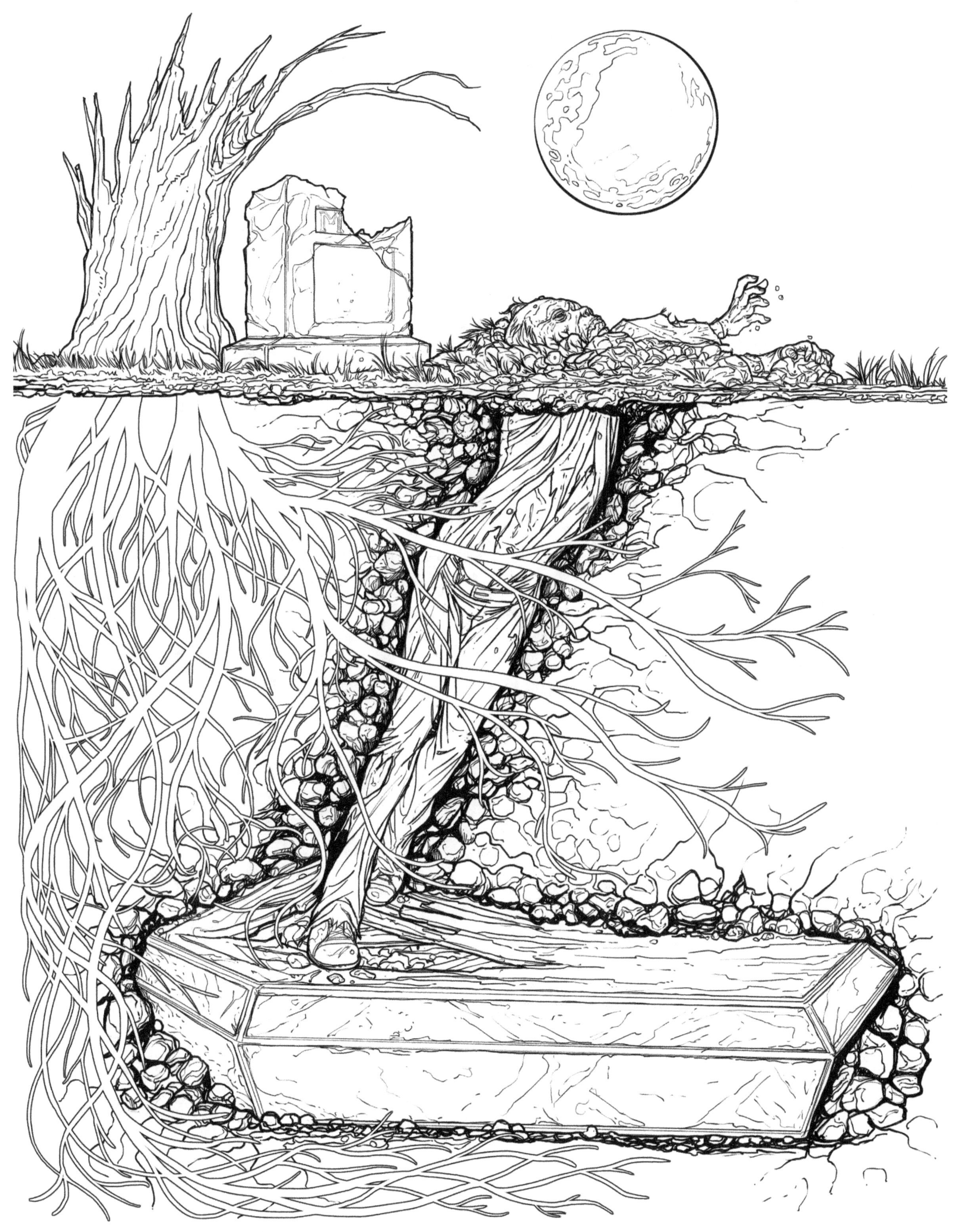

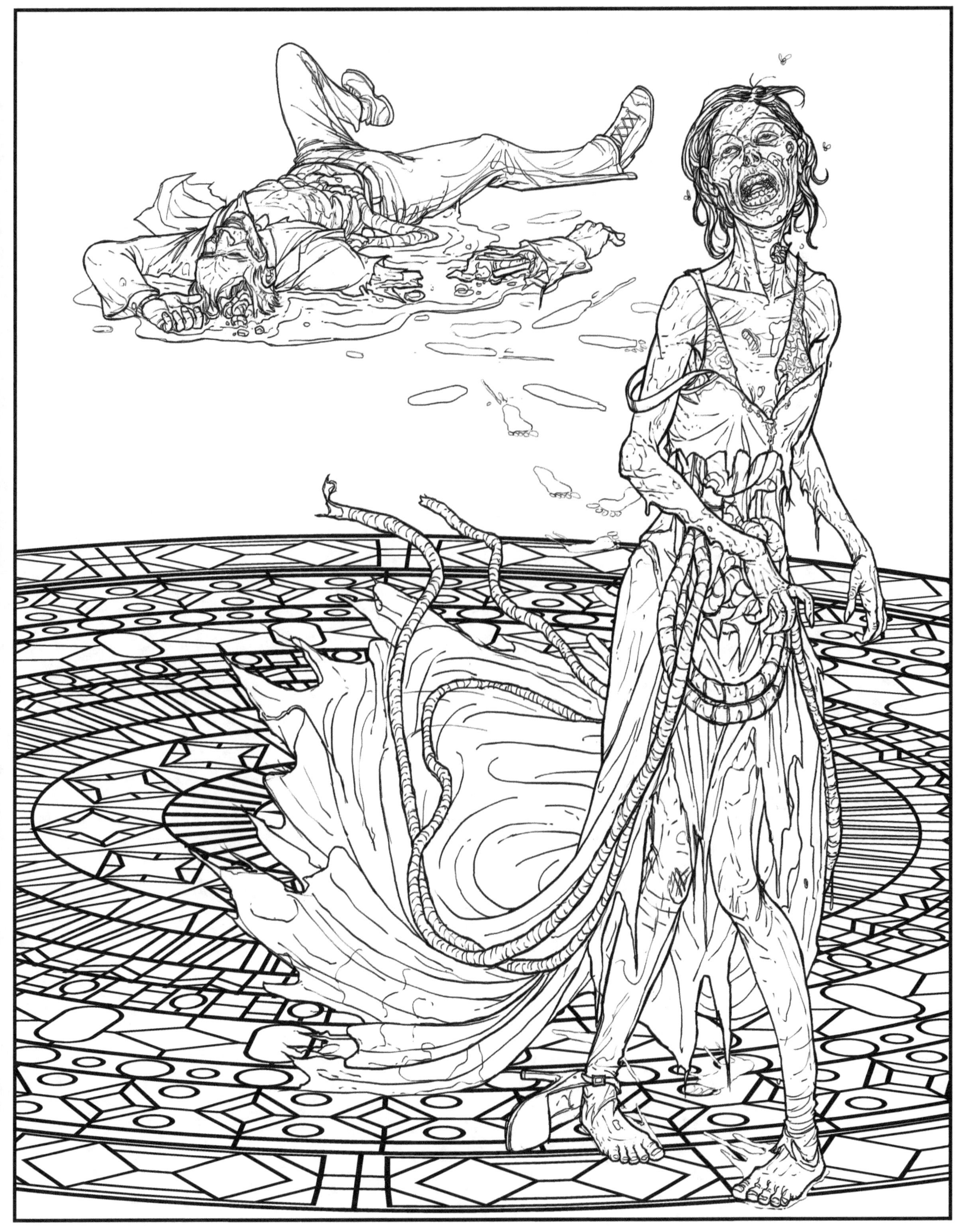

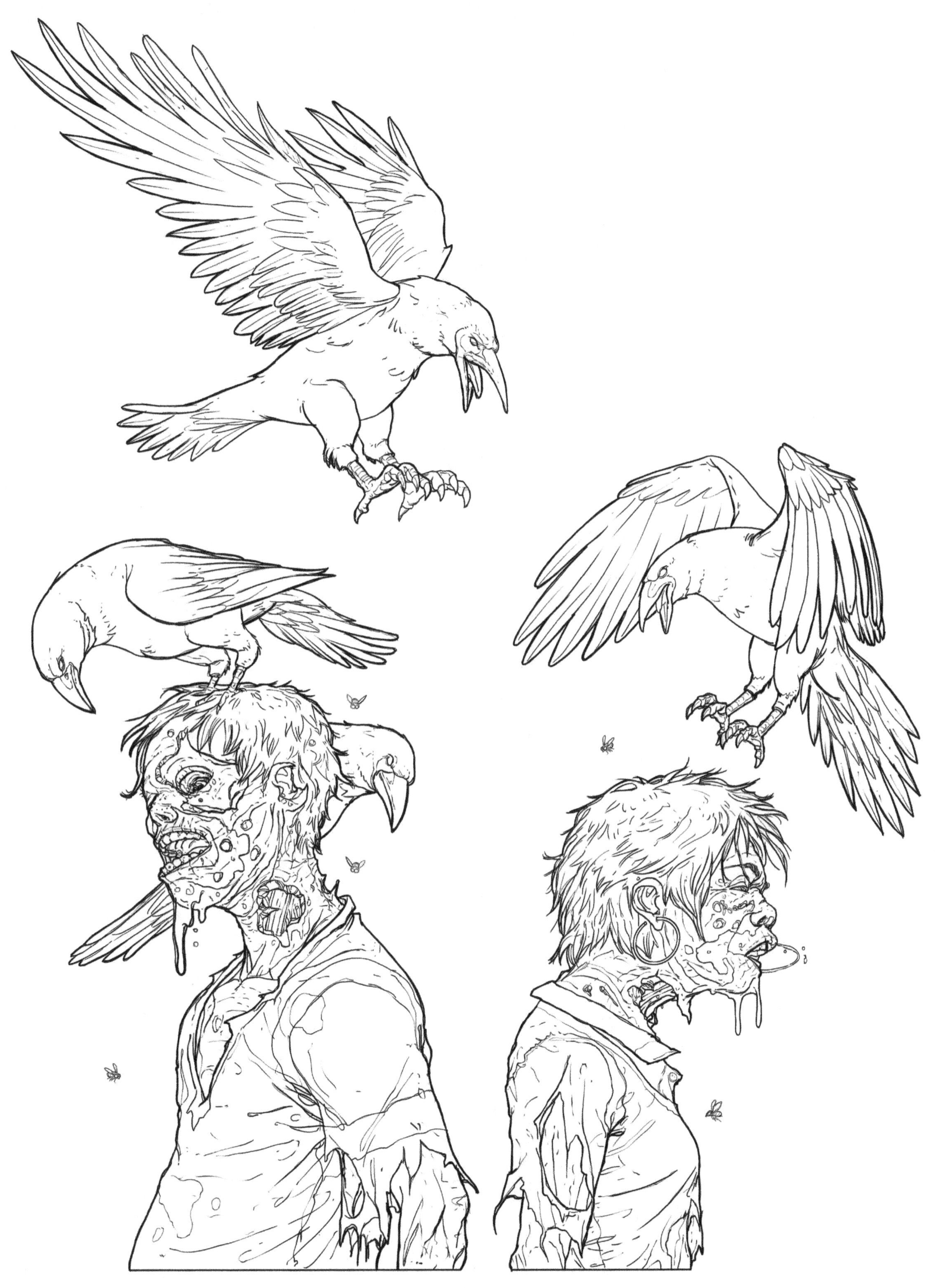

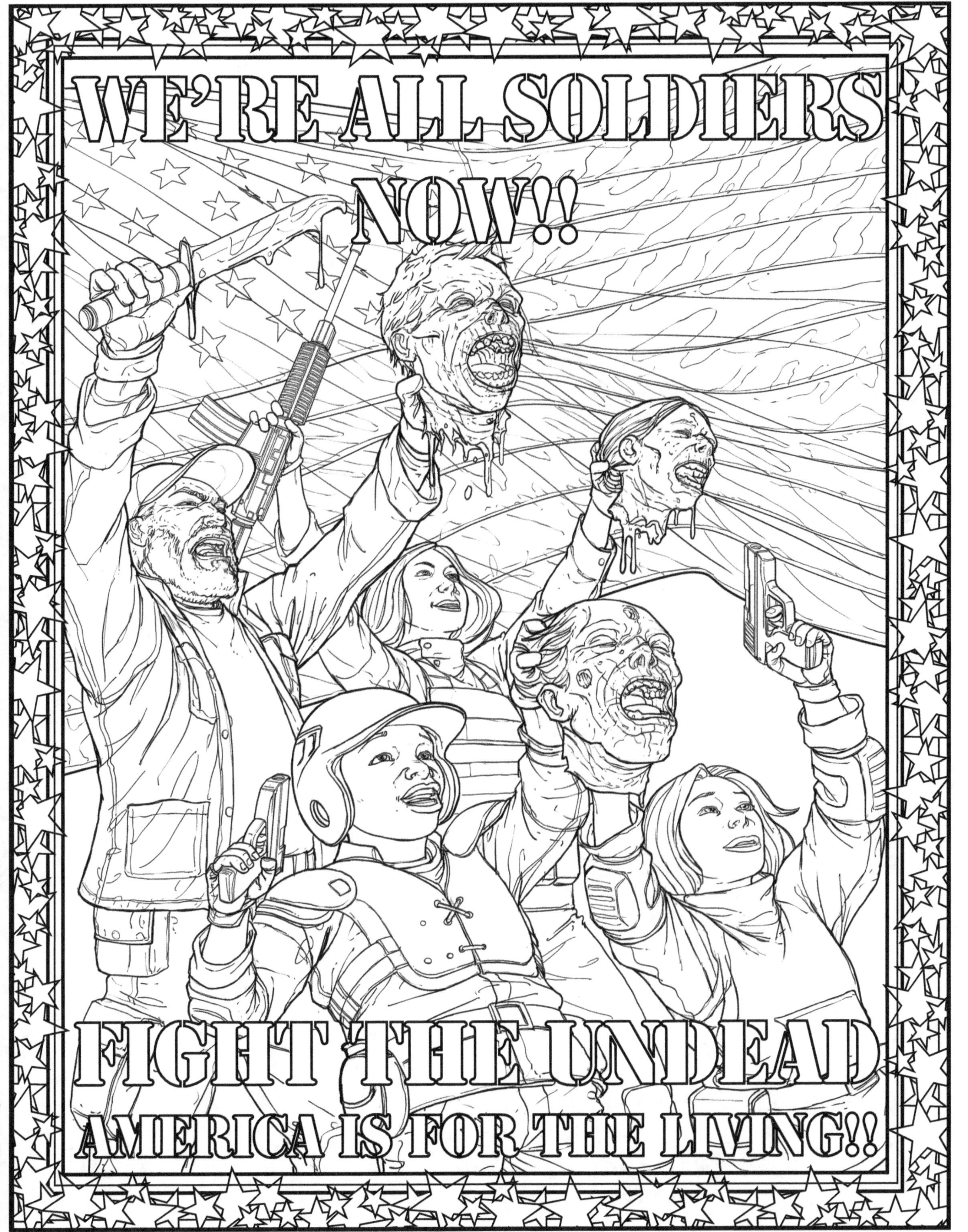

WE'RE ALL SOLDIERS NOW!!
FIGHT THE UNDEAD
AMERICA IS FOR THE LIVING!!

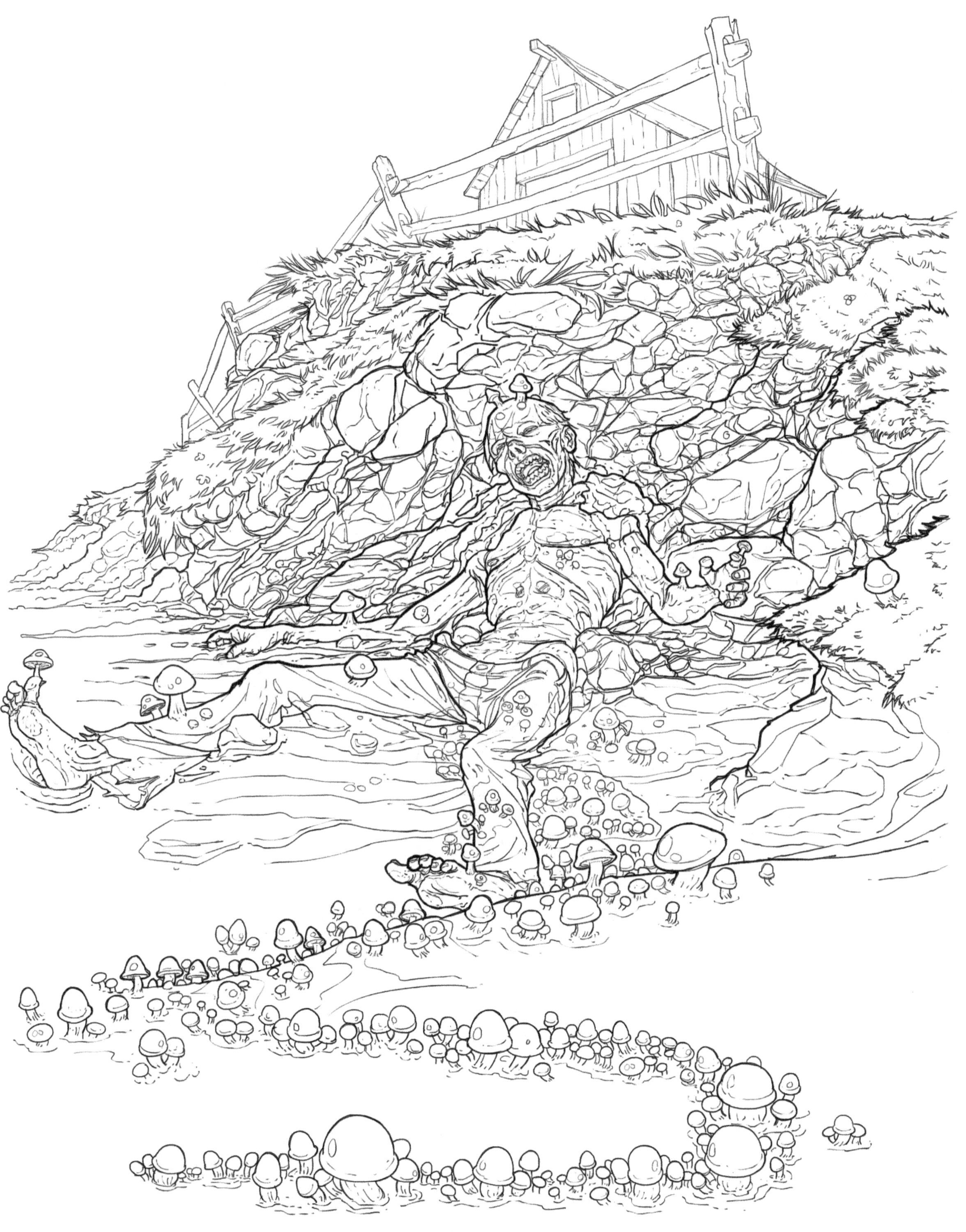

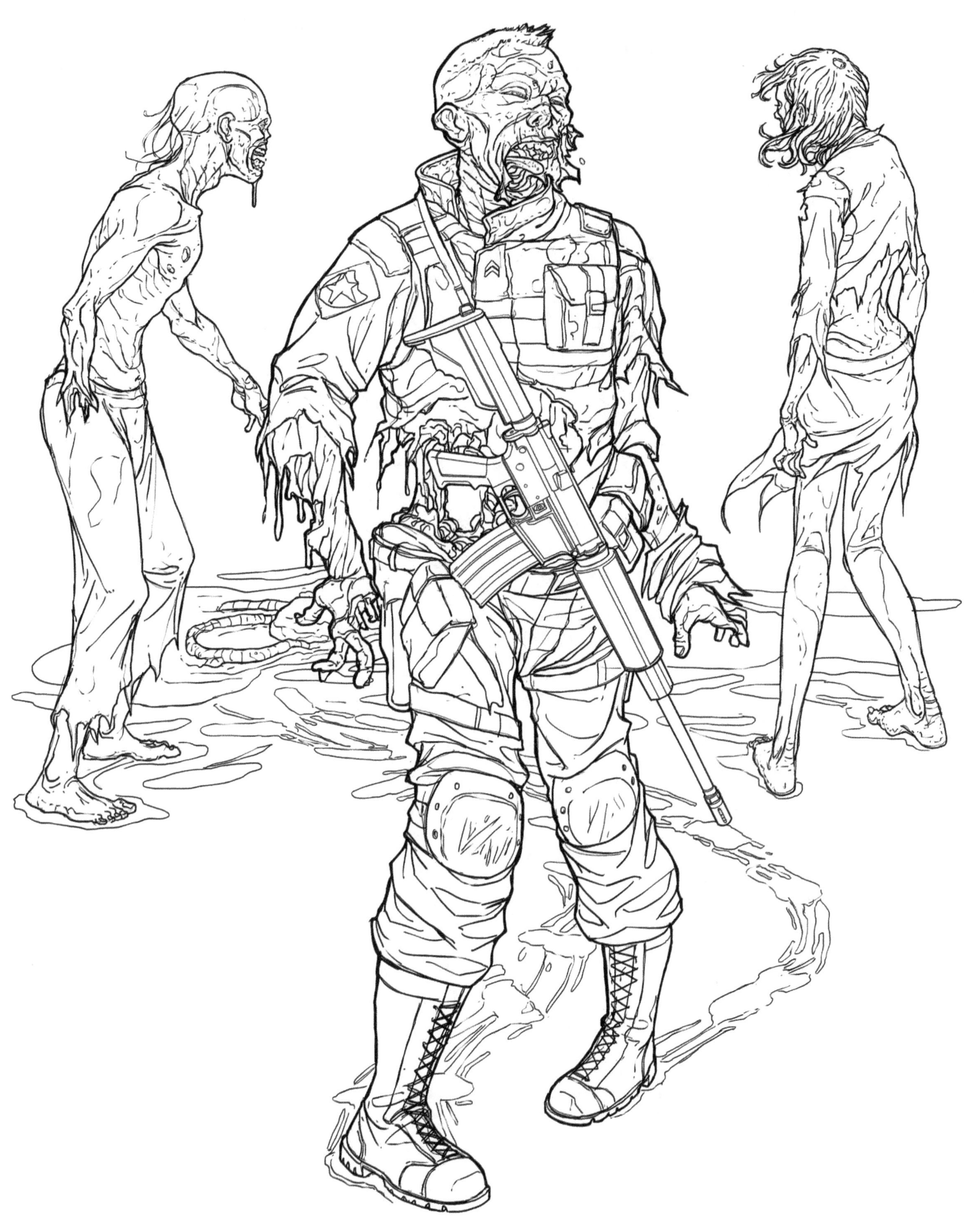

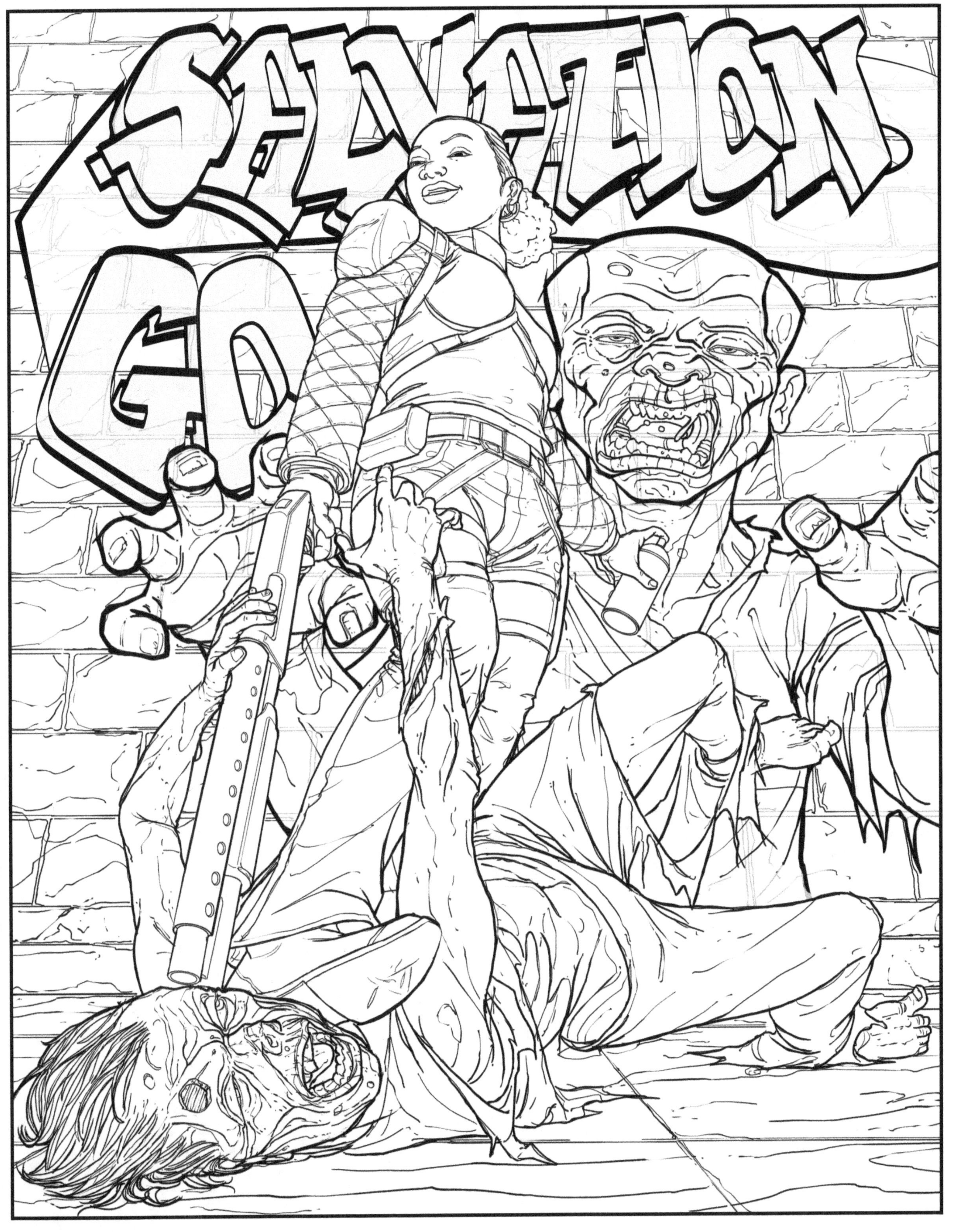

SALVATION
GO

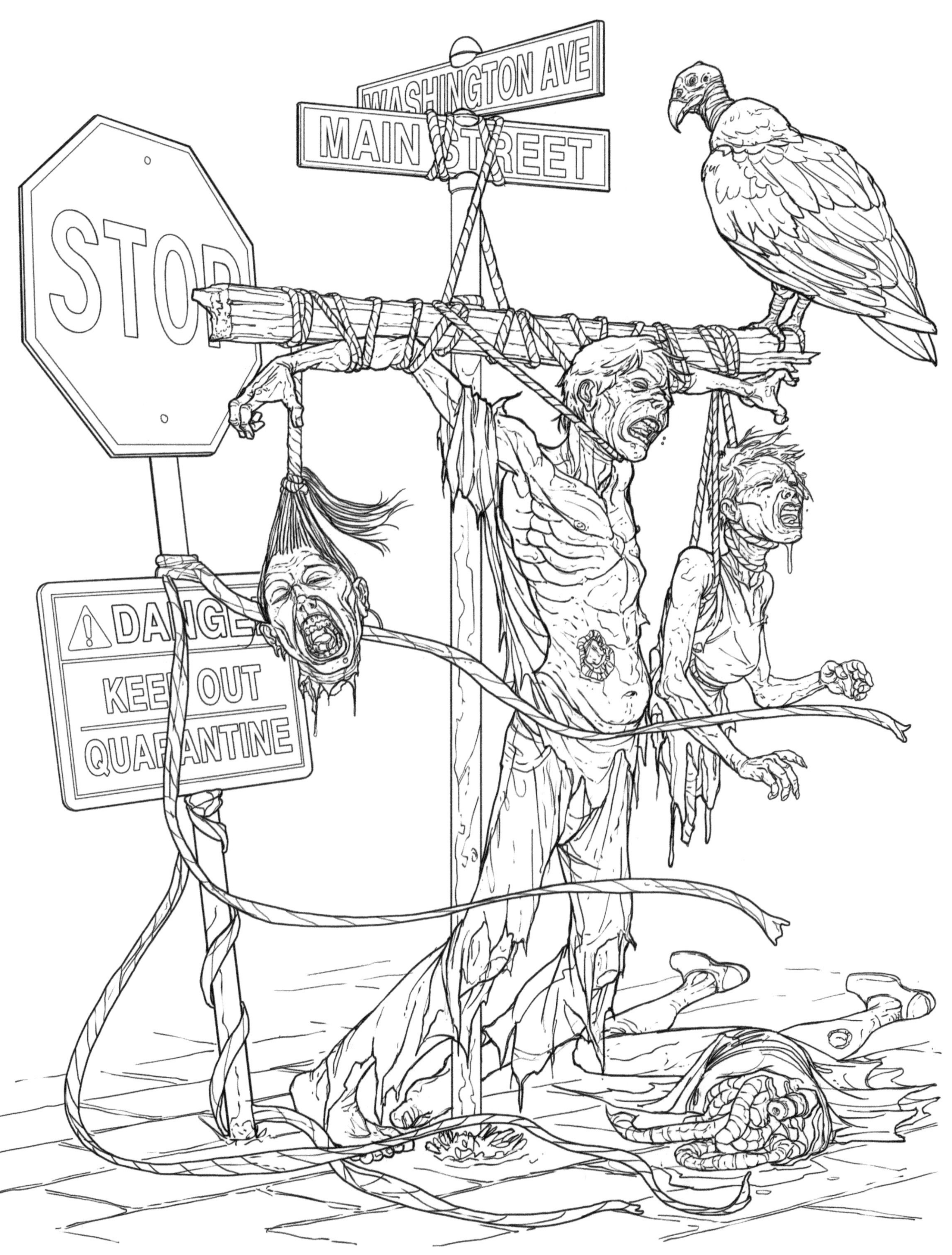

WASHINGTON AVE
MAIN STREET
STOP
DANGER
KEEP OUT
QUARANTINE

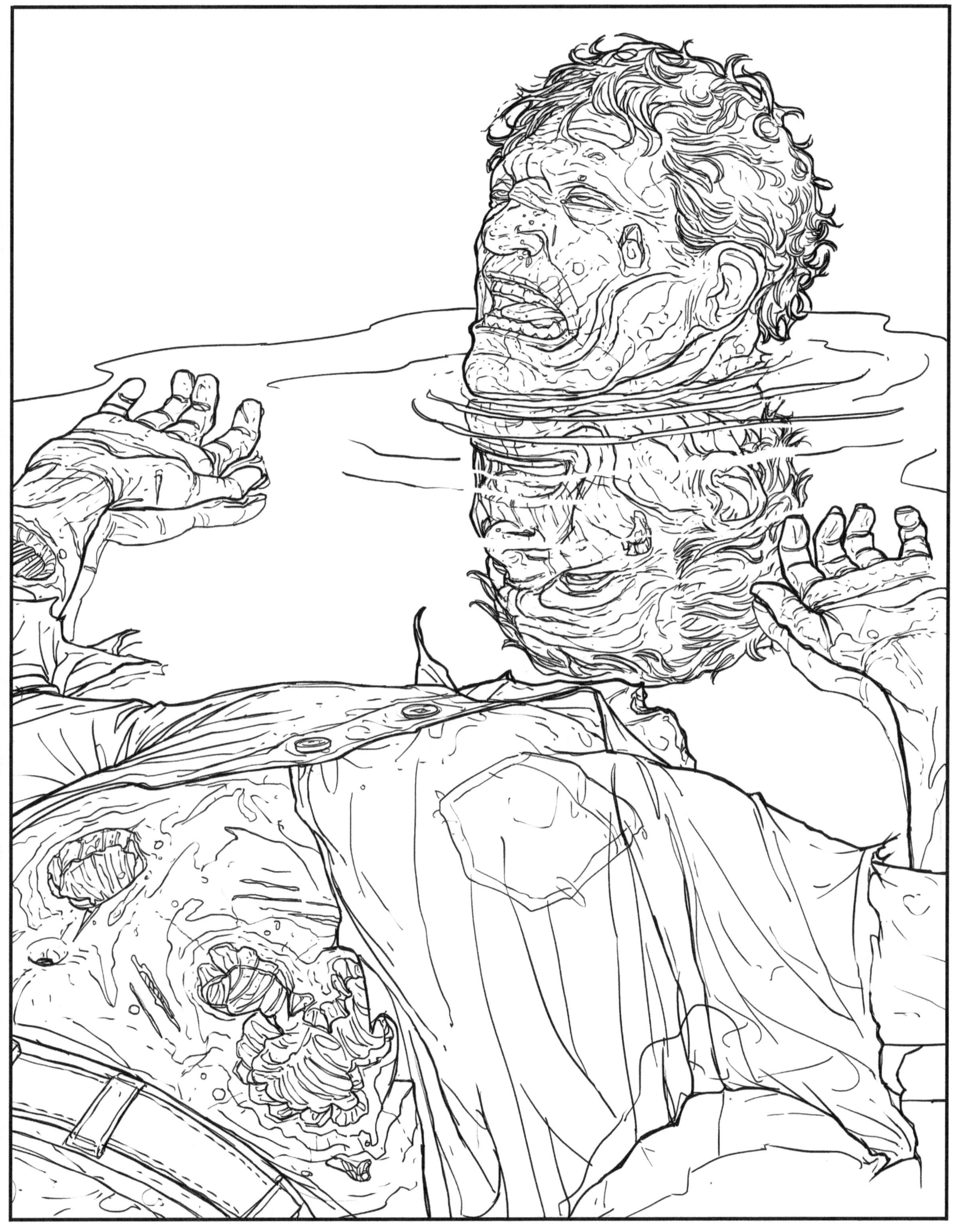

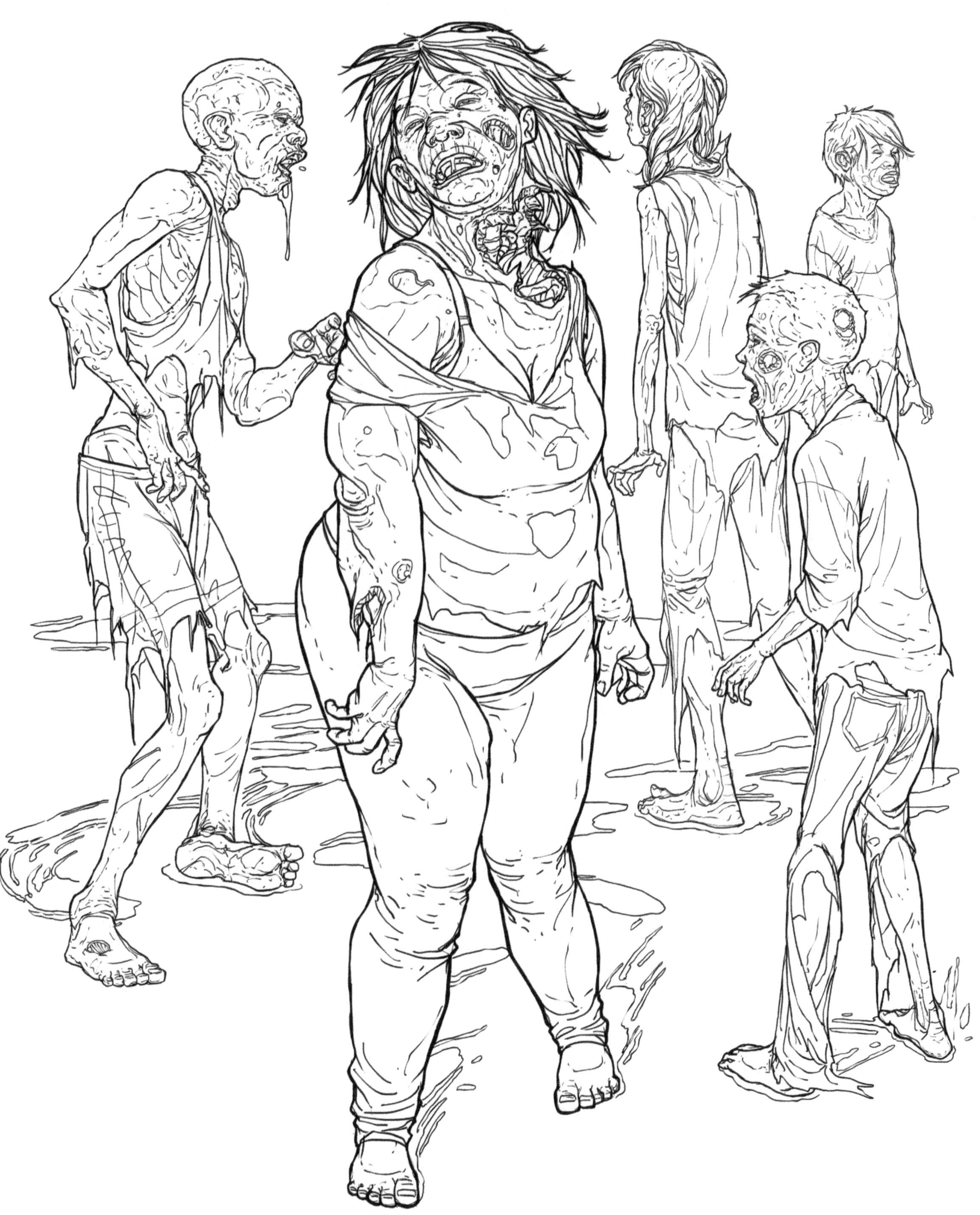

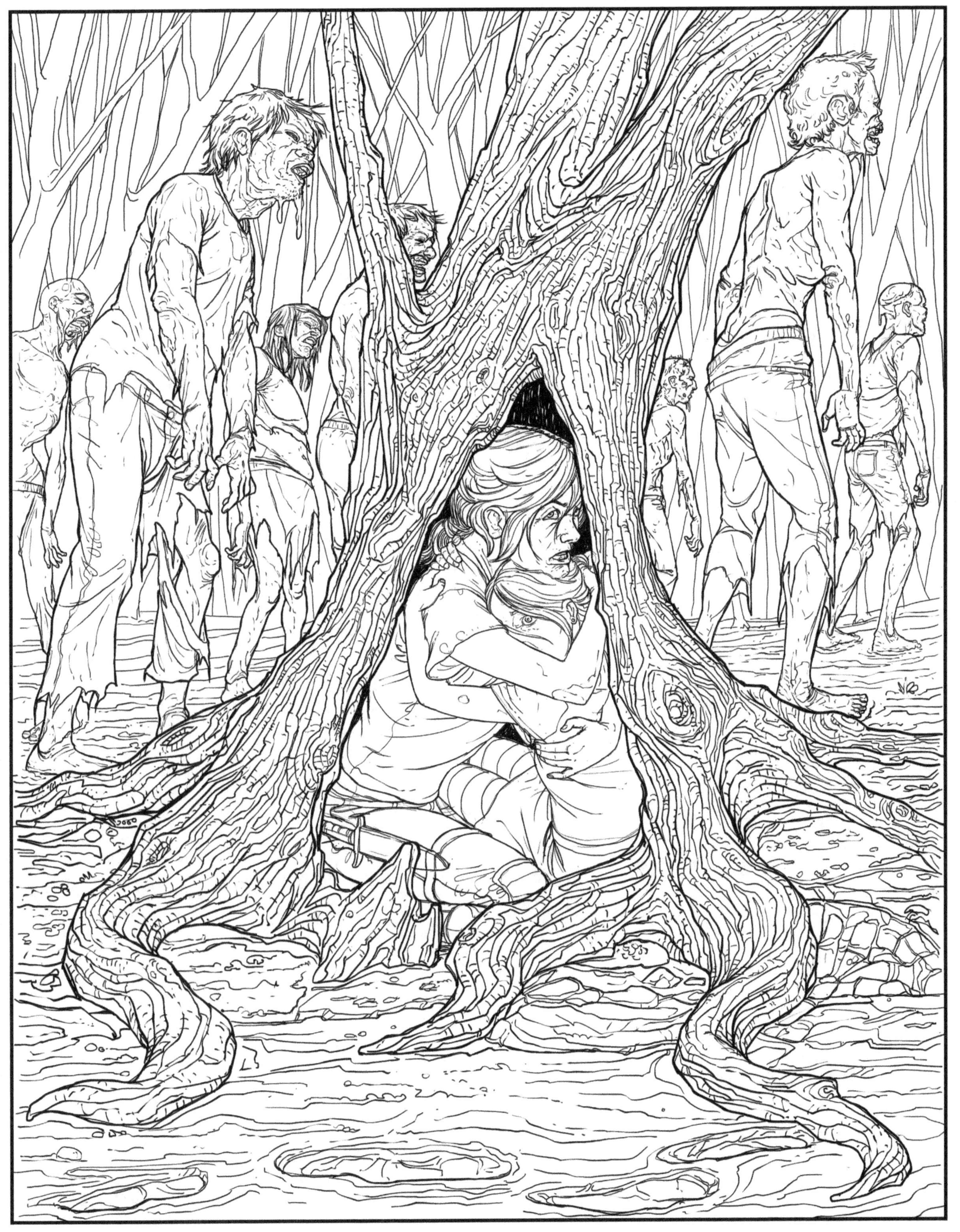

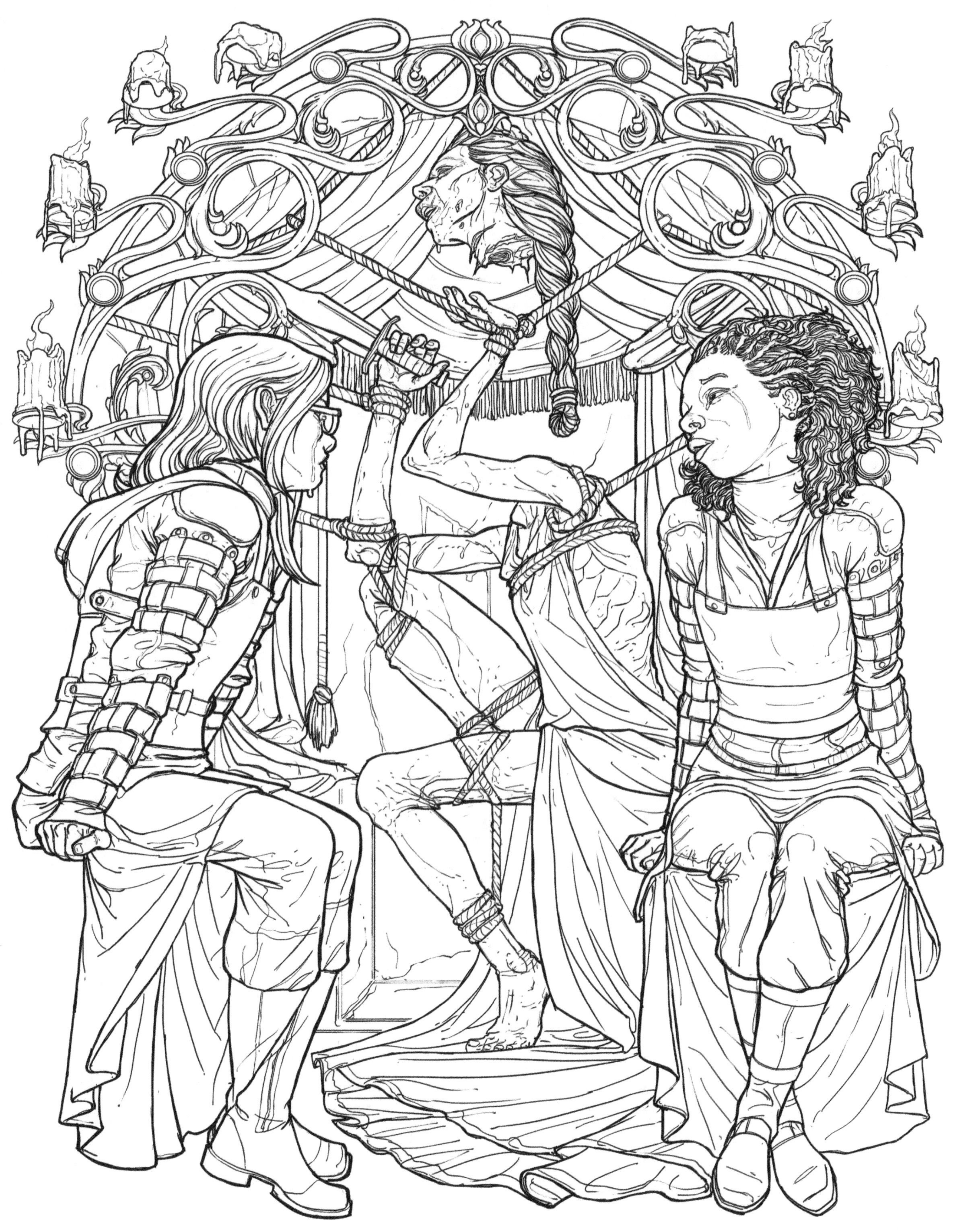

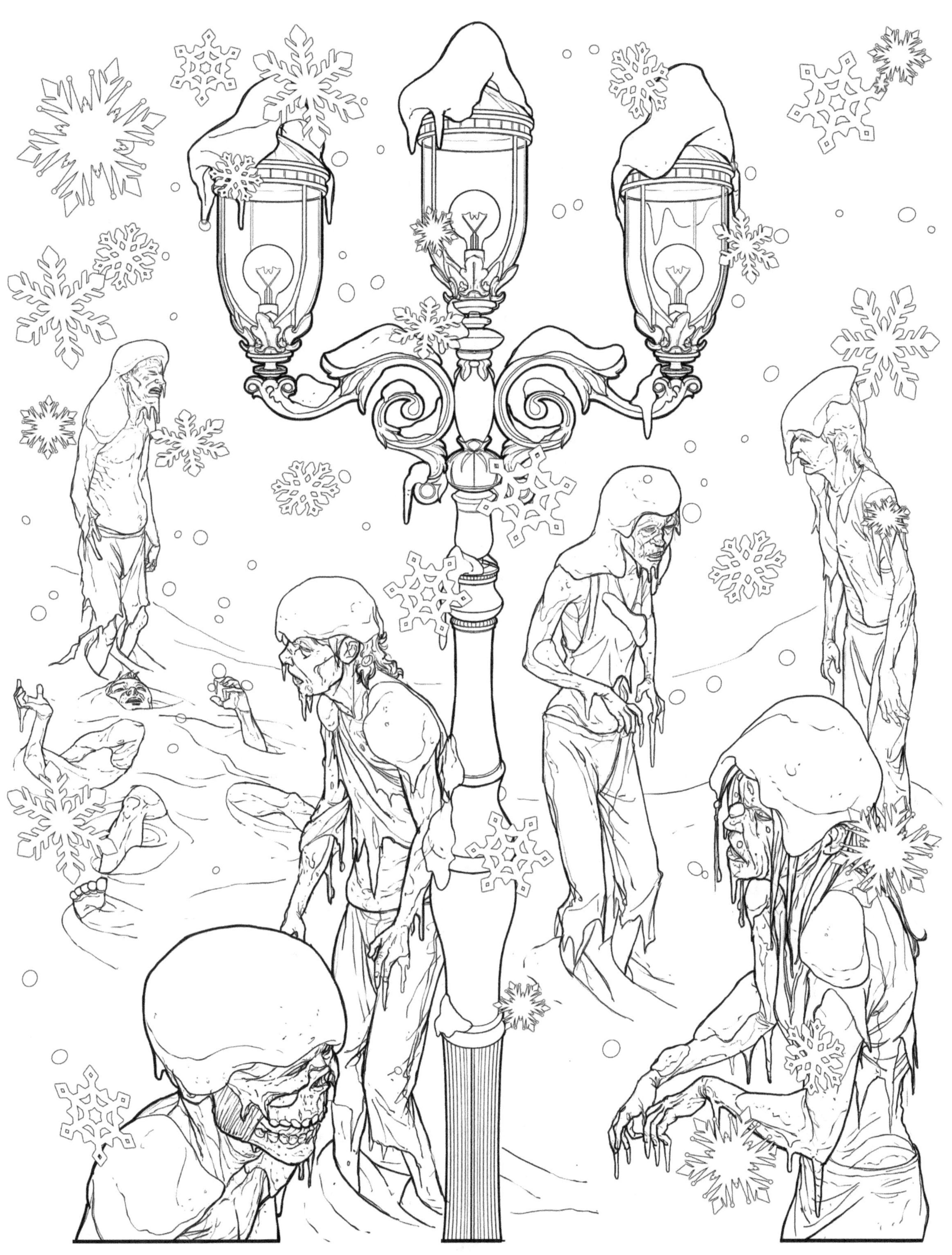

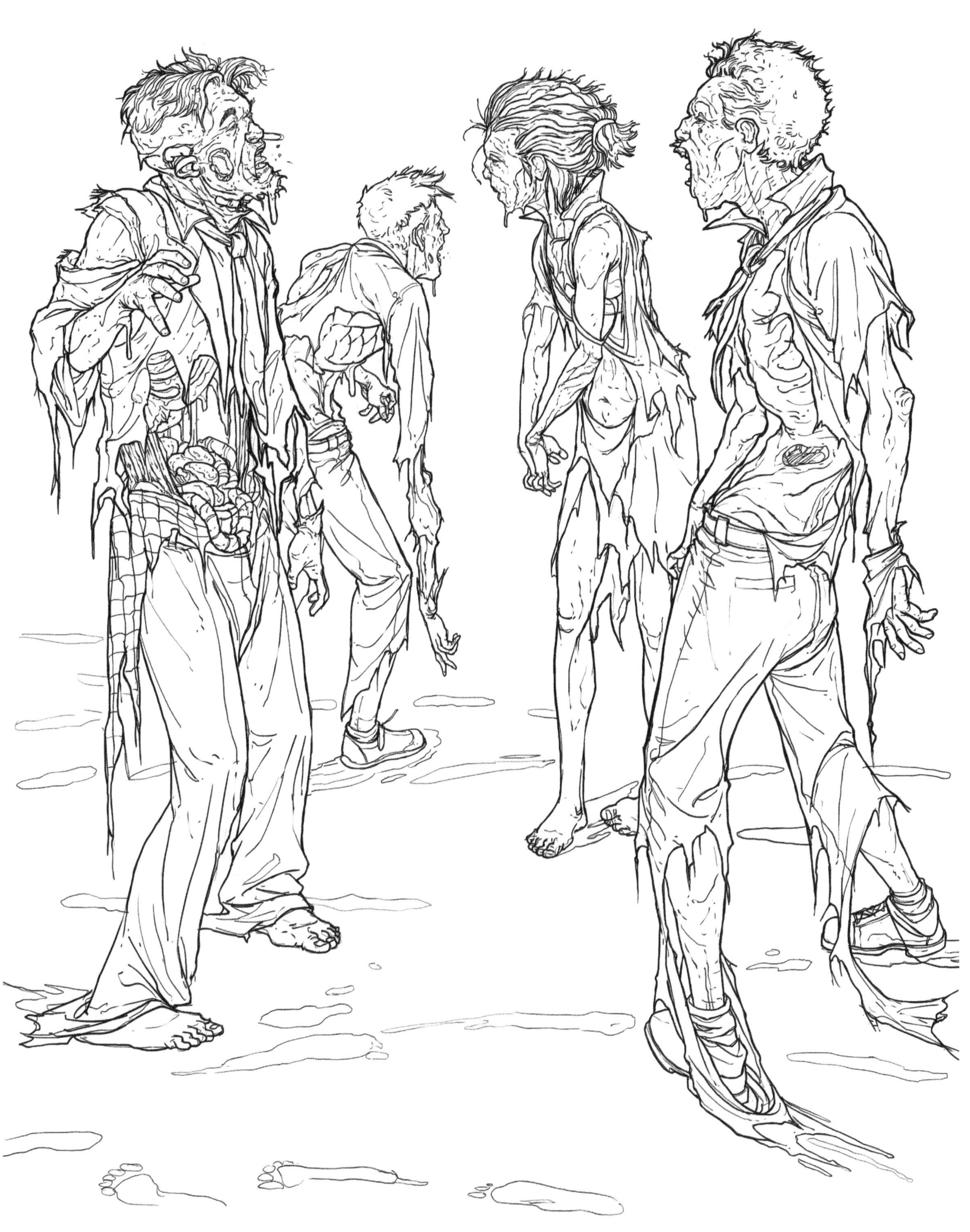

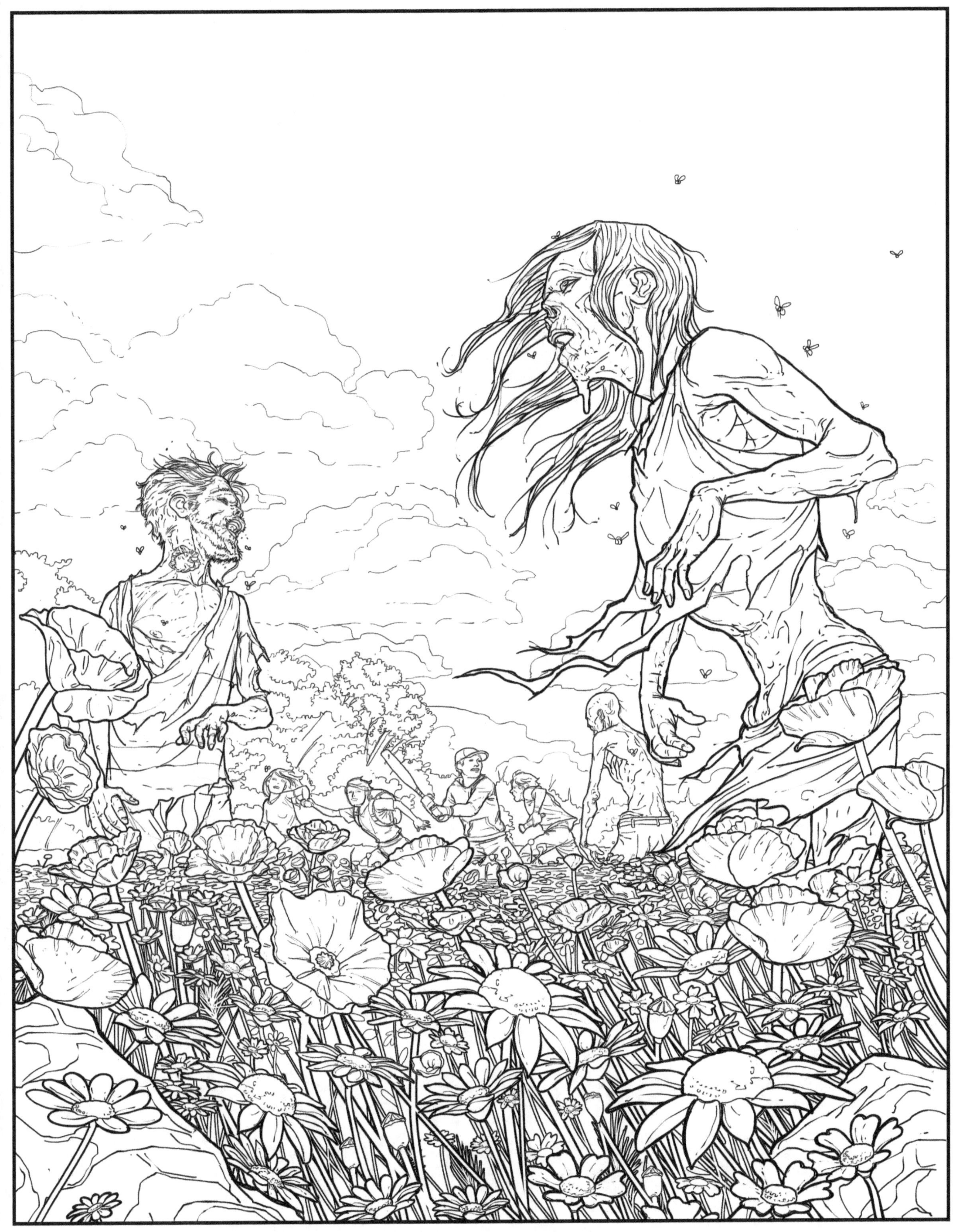

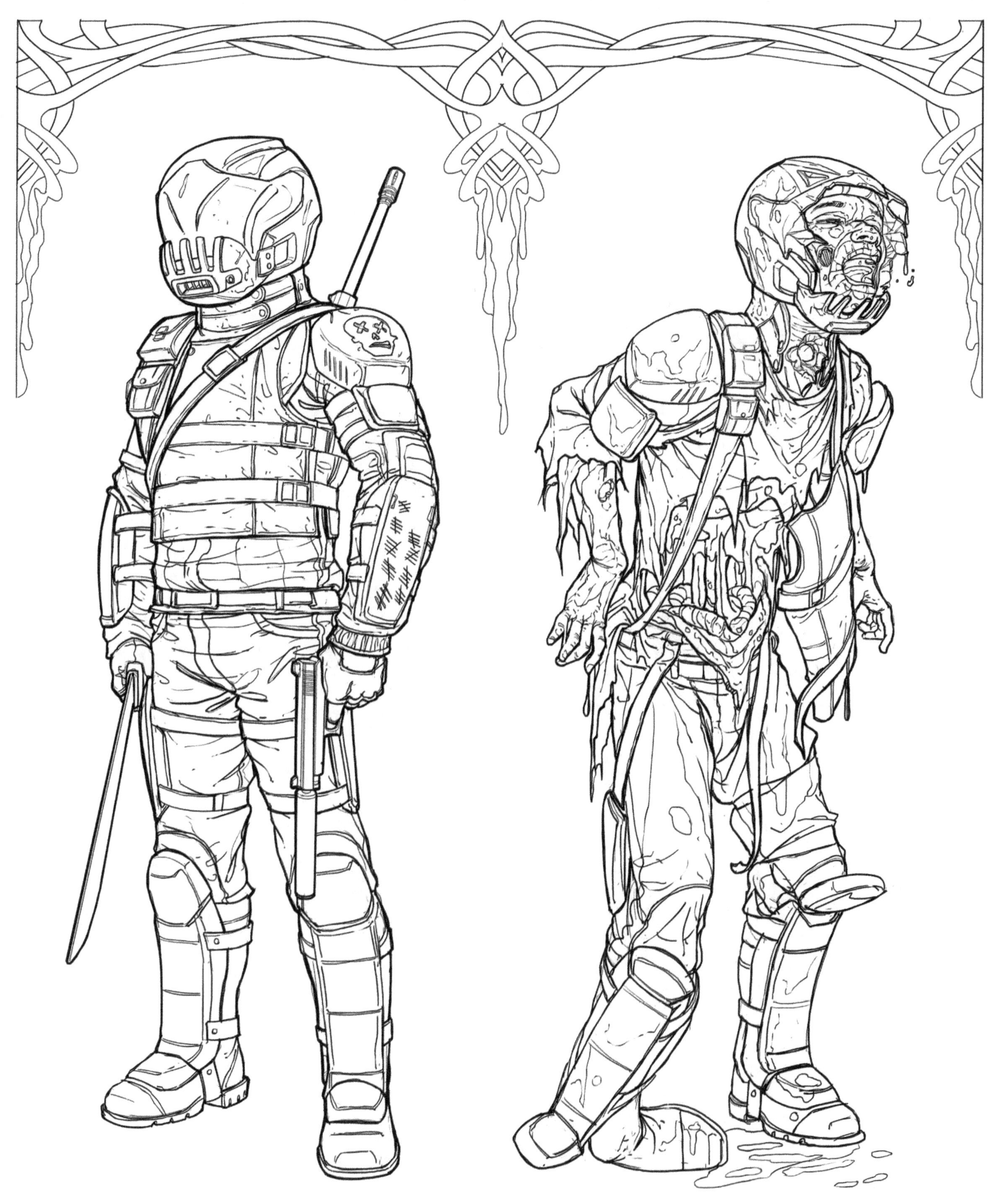

AUT VINCERE AUT MORI

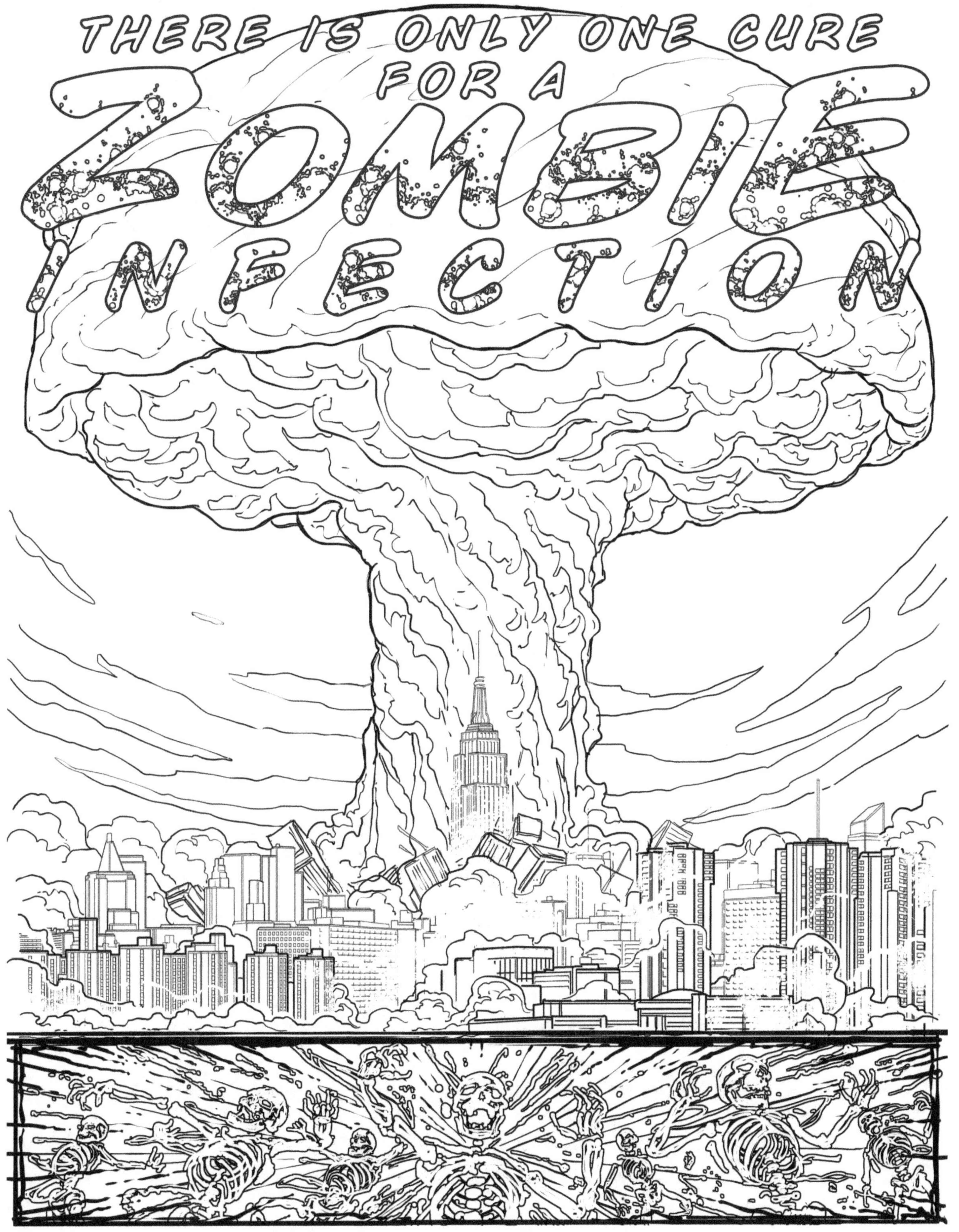

THERE IS ONLY ONE CURE
FOR A
ZOMBIE
INFECTION

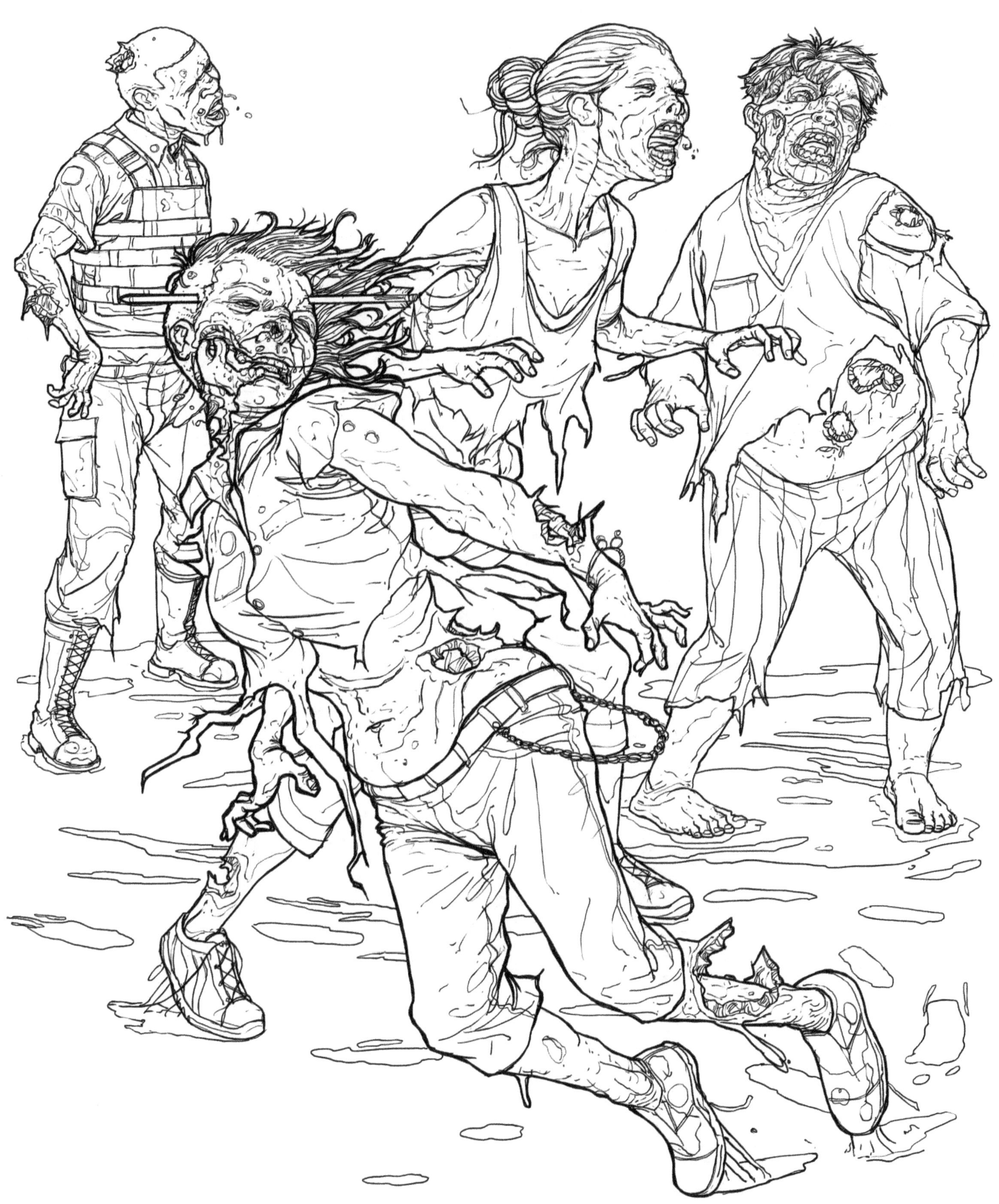

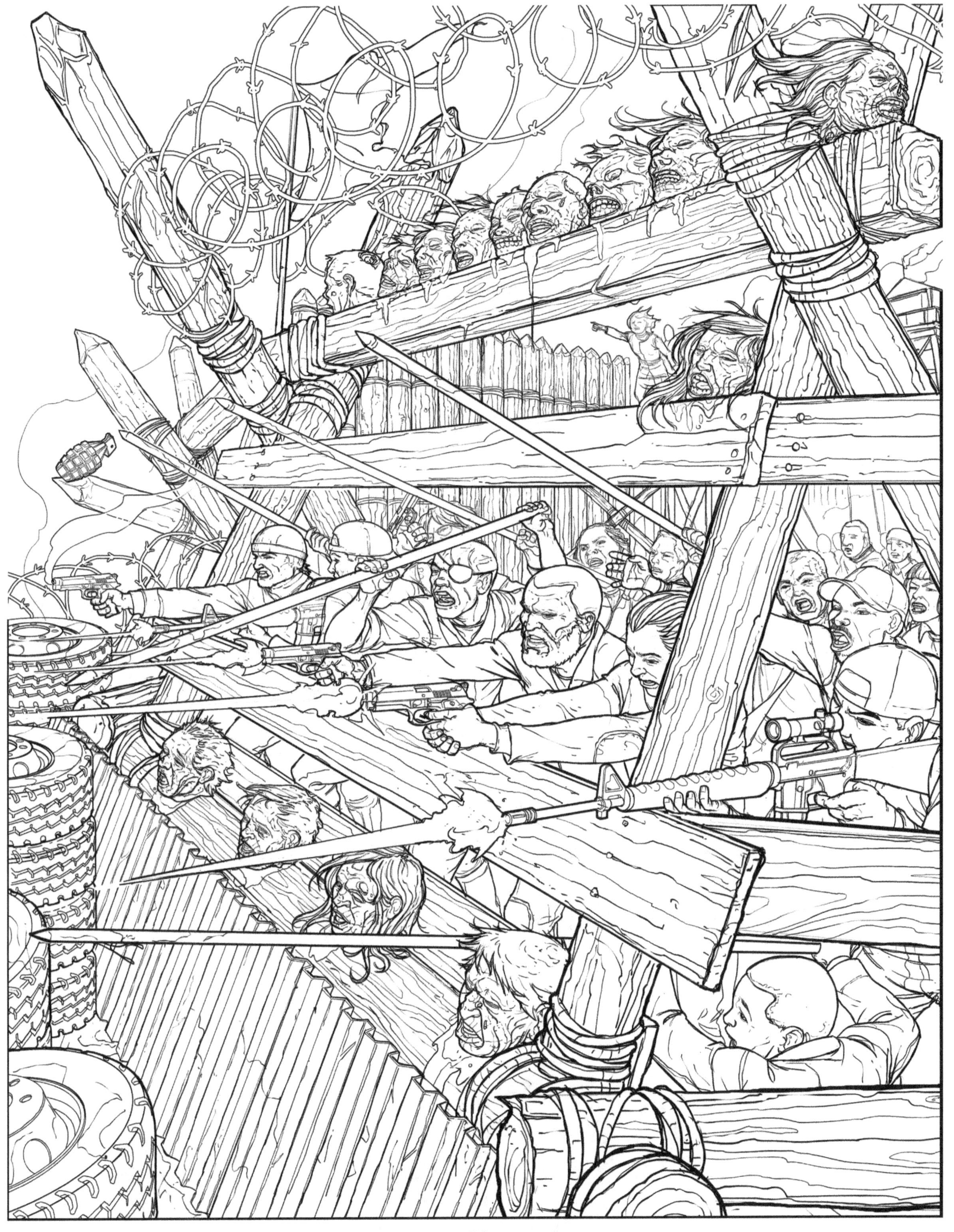

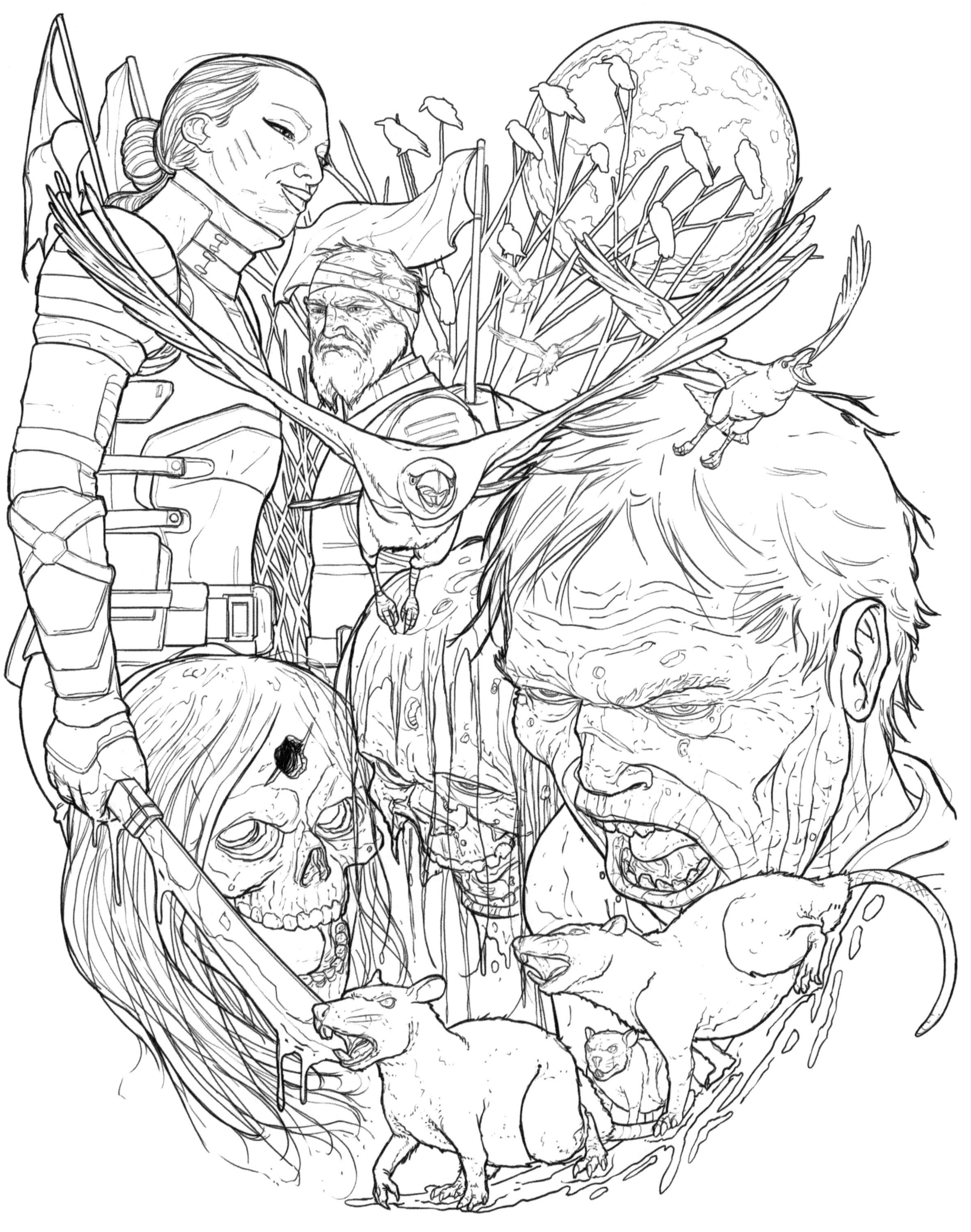

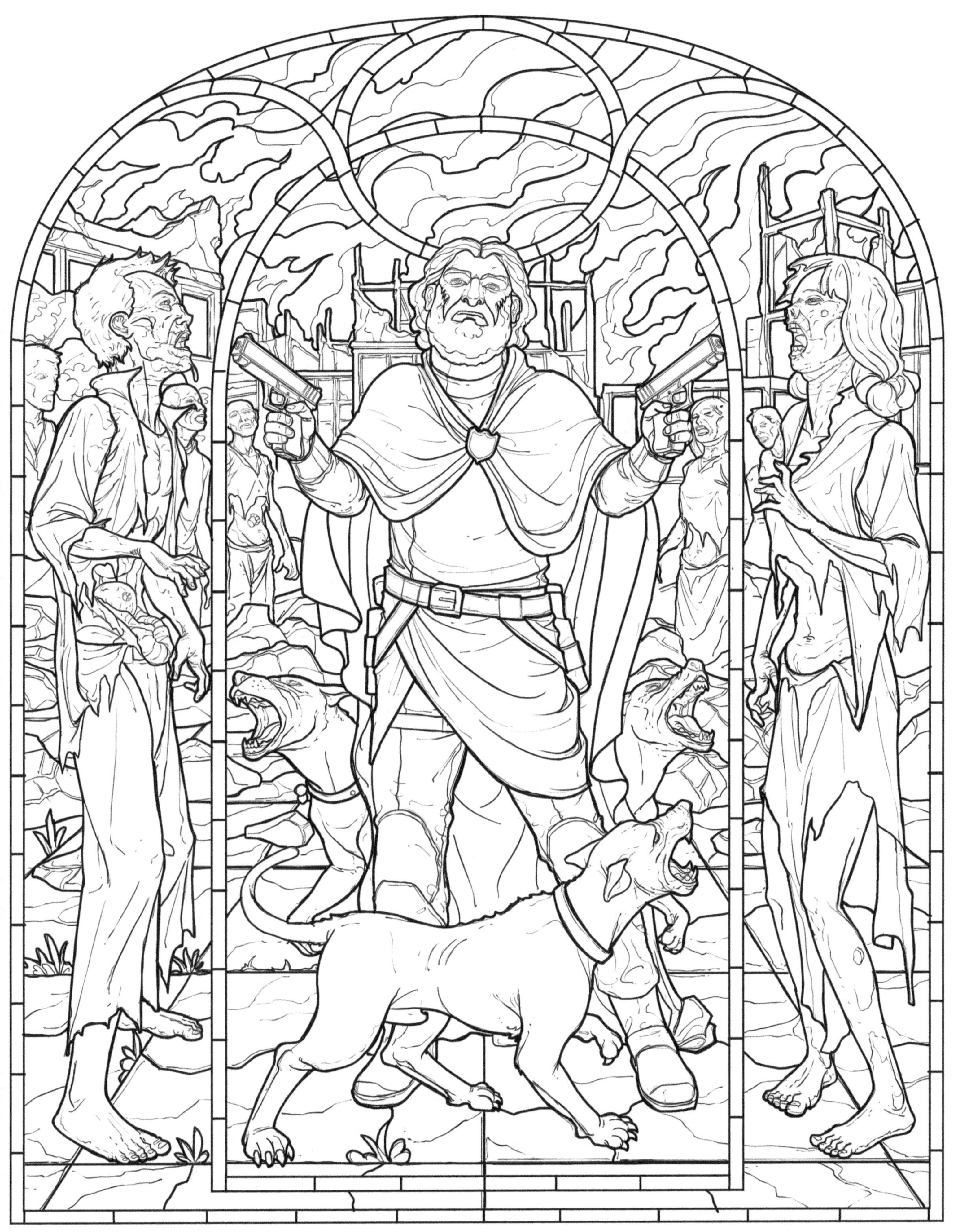

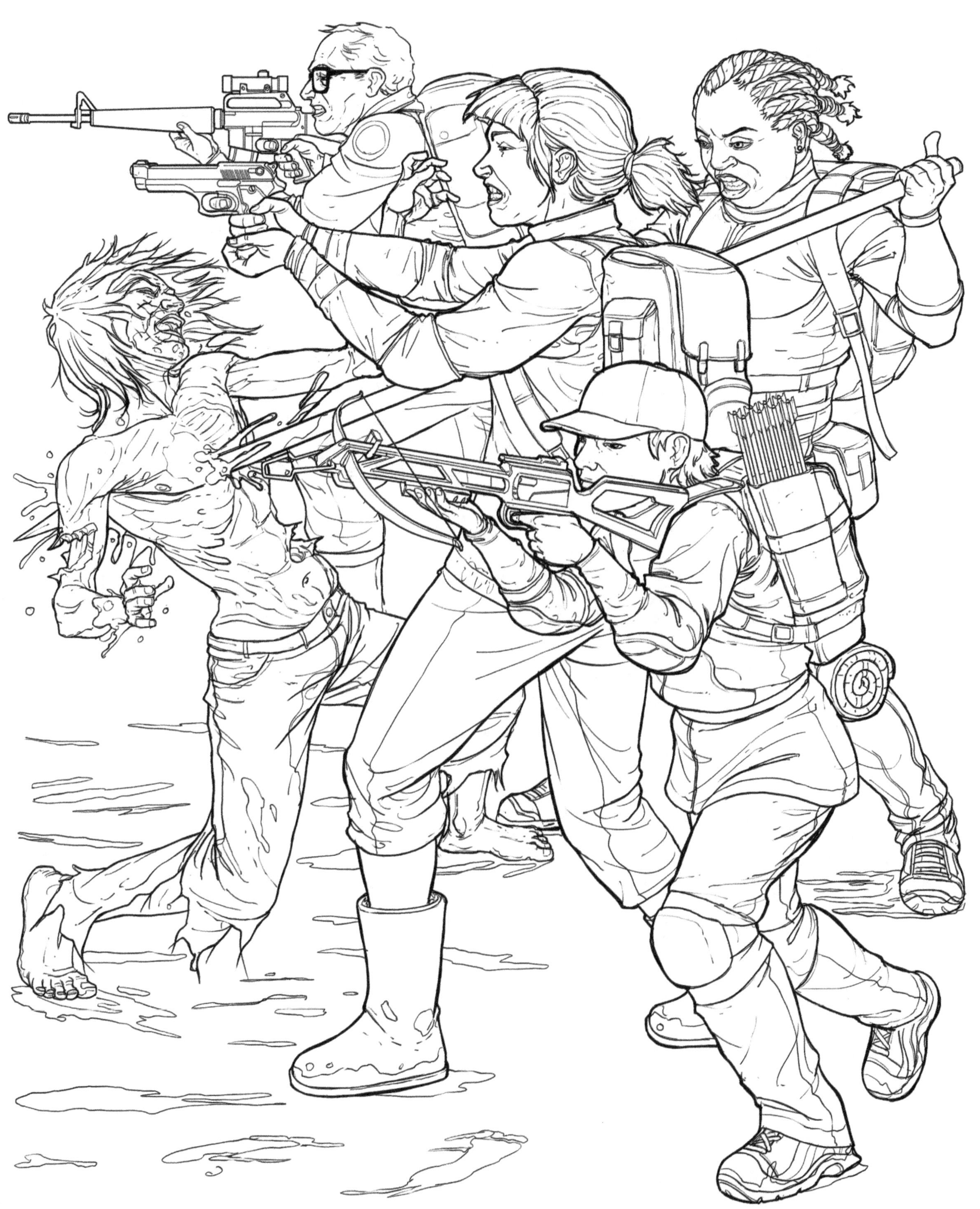